LADYBIRD BOOKS

UK | USA | Canada | Ireland | Australia
India | New Zealand | South Africa

Ladybird Books is part of the Penguin Random House group of companies
whose addresses can be found at global.penguinrandomhouse.com.
www.penguin.co.uk   www.puffin.co.uk   www.ladybird.co.uk

Penguin
Random House
UK

First published 2016
001

This book copyright © Astley Baker Davies Ltd/Entertainment One UK Ltd 2016
Adapted by Lauren Holowaty

This book is based on the TV series *Peppa Pig*.
Peppa Pig is created by Neville Astley and Mark Baker.
Peppa Pig © Astley Baker Davies Ltd/Entertainment One UK Ltd 2003.
www.peppapig.com

Printed in China

A CIP catalogue record for this book is available from the British Library

ISBN: 978-0-241-26280-1

All correspondence to:
Ladybird Books, Penguin Random House Children's
80 Strand, London, WC2R 0RL

Peppa's Christmas Post

It was nearly Christmas Eve, and Peppa and George were feeling very Christmassy.
"Let's post our letters to Santa!" said Peppa.
"Yippeeeee!" cheered George.

Peppa, George, Mummy and Daddy Pig put on their
boots and headed out into the snow to the postbox.

On the way home from the postbox, Daddy Pig did his Christmas dance. "Oh, it's a bit slipper-*wheeeee!*" he cried, falling on his bottom with a bump.

"Oh, Daddy Pig," said Mummy, holding out her hand to help him up. But then she slipped over, too!

Mummy and Daddy Pig were covered in snow.

Dr Brown Bear came to see if they were OK. "You're going to be fine," he said.

"But you've both had a bit of a bump, so you must rest until Christmas Day."
"Ohhhh no!" sighed Daddy Pig. Everybody went to stay at Granny and Grandpa Pig's house so Mummy and Daddy Pig could stay in bed.

"I know how we can cheer up Mummy and Daddy," Peppa whispered to George. "Let's get everything ready for Christmas ourselves!"
So, with a little help from Granny and Grandpa Pig, Peppa and George started making Christmas cards and advent calendars for everyone they knew.

After Peppa and George posted everything they had made, it was time to make the Christmas pudding.

"Mummy and Daddy will love this!" said Peppa, stirring the sticky mixture.

"That looks perfect, little ones," said Granny Pig. "Let's steam it, and then I have something to show you!"

Granny Pig found an envelope in a drawer
and passed it to Peppa and George.
"Take a look inside," she said.
"Oooooh!" said Peppa. "Thank you, Granny!"

Granny Pig
Old Cottage
The Knoll

Inside the envelope was a *Little Book of Festive Treats*.

Peppa and George made all of the recipes in it, and a lot of mess!

"Hmmmm! Something smells delicious," said Grandpa Pig, his tummy rumbling.
"They're not for now, Grandpa," explained Peppa. "They're for Christmas Day."
"I see," replied Grandpa Pig. "Well then, I can't wait for Christmas Day!"

"What's in that great big box, Grandpa?" asked Peppa. "Christmas decorations!" said Grandpa Pig.

"Hooray! Let's decorate the Christmas tree," cheered Peppa.

FRAGILE

↑THIS WAY UP↑

Peppa and George covered the whole house with Grandpa Pig's decorations! "Mummy and Daddy are going to be very surprised when they come downstairs on Christmas Day!" cried Peppa.

Then she and George sat down with Granny Pig. They wanted to write an extra-special letter to Santa.

Peppa, George, Granny and Grandpa Pig put on their boots and headed out into the snow to post their special letter. "I hope Santa gets it in time," said Peppa, lifting George up so he could post the letter.

"I'm sure he will, Peppa," said Grandpa Pig.
"Come on, let's head back home."

Santa Claus
The North Pole

That night at the North Pole, Santa Claus received Peppa and George's special letter. "Ho, ho, ho!" he laughed. "Christmas stickers – how lovely!"

Then he got out his pen and paper and wrote an extra-special reply.

The next morning was Christmas Eve and there was a letter waiting for Peppa and George by the front door.

"Someone's written us a letter, George!" said Peppa, jumping up and down.

"San-ta!" cheered George.

"Don't be silly, George," replied Peppa. "Santa doesn't write letters. He's too busy making toys."

Peppa and George Pig
Old Cottage
The Knoll

Of cou

mummy

bed nice and

there will be an

you both on Ch

Love t

FROM SANTA

At bedtime on Christmas Eve, Peppa and George were soon tucked up in their little bed at Granny and Grandpa's house.

"We have to go to sleep early like Santa said in his letter," whispered Peppa. "I wonder what his surprise will be?"

"San-ta," whispered George, as he closed his eyes. Soon, they were both fast asleep.

"Mummy! Daddy!" cheered Peppa and George very early the next morning. "It's Christmas Day!"
"Eh! Who? What?" mumbled Daddy Pig, waking up.

"It's Christmas Day," repeated Peppa. "Dr Brown Bear said you can get out of bed now! We have lots of surprises for you."

But there was a surprise waiting for EVERYONE in the living room . . .
"Santa!" cried Peppa and George.
"Santa!" cried Daddy Pig, doing his special Christmas dance very carefully
this time and managing not to fall over.
"Surprise!" said Santa. "I thought I'd pop in and see two little piggies
who have been very helpful this Christmas . . ."

"... Peppa and George!"

"Hooray!" cheered Peppa and George.
Santa gave presents to Mummy and Daddy Pig, and to Granny and Grandpa Pig. Then he turned to Peppa and George and gave them the doll and the racing car they had asked for!
"Ho, ho, ho! Merry Christmas!" he chuckled as he waved goodbye.
"Now, remember to write your thank-you letters . . . I love getting post!"

That night, Peppa and George were back at home and tucked up in their own beds.

"I love getting post, too, Santa," whispered Peppa, looking at his letter on her bedroom wall. "Especially from you!"

6 1 2 6 1 2 6 1 2

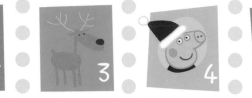

4 5 3 4 5 3 4 5 3

1 2 4 1 2 4 1 2 4

6 1 2 6 1 2 6 1 2

4 5 3 4 5 3 4 5 3

1 2 4 1 2 4 1 2 4